NICKY - A BIT OF A WET RAG

NICKY - A BIT OF A WET RAG

What goes on behind the curtain of a closet Homosexual

Julian Black

authorHOUSE®

AuthorHouse™ UK Ltd.
1663 Liberty Drive
Bloomington, IN 47403 USA
www.authorhouse.co.uk
Phone: 0800.197.4150

Published by AuthorHouse 07/28/2014

ISBN: 978-1-4969-8787-7 (sc)
ISBN: 978-1-4969-8789-1 (e)

This book is printed on acid-free paper.

This is not a document or paper on closetry but a story of closetry.

Sexuality is only a problem if you feel you need to hide it.

When the question was put to me in my teens, twenties and early thirties "Why won't you come out?" I never knew the answer. It suddenly dawned on me one day what the answer to this puzzling question was. The answer was: I do not know how to be happy and I do not know how to live without fear in my life, for me to be happy and for me to live without fear is more frightening to me than fear itself, simply because fear was a huge part of me.

-Nicky

A lot of people around the world do not understand homosexuality or the LGBT community, and do not want or wish to understand it. I wonder if they feel the same about closetry.

Closetry is a lot like choking. Choking on the air you breathe especially when resentment comes into it towards others having fun and just living their lives.

To be afraid is human but we should never let fear take control of us.

Grace Sheppard: An aspect of fear.

I was a strange child even from the very start I was one of four siblings and all boys and I was very different to the others you just know when you are different because it's the way people treat you and look at you and you just know yourself that you are not the ' norm ' whatever the norm is I was just different from my brothers and many others and did they notice it. I think the strangeness starts from an early age or at least it did in my case anyway I would not conform to what is expected of a young boy like playing sports or going out with friends or being part of something or belonging to the world we live on and having an Identity as a young boy having fun.

I was a very emotional child and I can remember my first day of a brand new school and where the other kids in the class were socialising and laughing and getting to know each other I was sat on my own hugging my pencil case and crying to myself feeling sorry for myself and just making no effort to go and join in on the fun. This is where the other kids get to know you and judge you straight away it's very rare to get two of the same kids like me in the same class and I guess this is where the Isolation starts and the feeling that you are all alone and have nobody to relate too. (This is where life gets difficult from a very early age for people like me).

I spent my childhood being afraid of the world which we all live on because I was different and people treated me as different even my own family I was mocked a lot and made fun of a lot as I say because I was just different my mother over protected me because she could see the sadness in my eyes and my brothers knew that she favoured me more than them.

In school my brothers kept away from me and were kind of embarrassed of me being related to them and I would hear their friends saying "how are you and him from the same family" and I would hear them responding by saying "I don't know myself", when we got home from school around the dinner table my brothers would say to mum and dad that I should make more of an effort to fit in around school and act "normal" because they were getting a lot of hassle from their friends about me being so strange.

I had one or two friends in school and believe it or not they used to come over to my house and I used to go to their house and we used to go walking as friends and camp out as friends in our own tents. But it came to a point where I stopped going out and those few friends I had stopped calling for me I guess I just gave up on life and I cannot tell you why simply because I do not know what happened myself. (I guess I just got depressed at a very early age and stopped living).

My dad would just look at me with a long stare and disappointed look and told me to get a life and stop acting so pathetic and girly and to be more like my brothers which did the world of good to my confidence and self - esteem if I ever had any at all, my mother would just look at me and say "be who ever you want to be" and my dad would say to her "look it's that kind of molly coddle attitude from you that is making the boy as he is" as you can imagine I hated the dinner table and I hated the house I lived in apart from my mother of course but I always felt as if she was not strong enough a person to stand her ground where she was concerned or where I was concerned with a house full of testosterone and macho men who liked their opinions and attitudes to be heard.

I always enjoyed it when they were not around and it was just me and mum this was the time when I could just relax and be myself my mother was comfortable with me being different to the others and I always felt I could be myself around her and just let go of the pretence of living up to my fathers and brothers image because when they were around it was just a false pretence lifestyle and me having to be somebody else.

I was nothing like my brothers I was not macho I did not leave my room in a tip I did not leave my room smell of odour and dirty socks and pants with dirty skid marks that stood up on their own for all the family to see, and I did not have a bed that stunk of beer and bad breath and stale farts, I did not have posters on my walls of naked girls or the latest pin up model and I did not have all the top quality clothes and all the latest fashion in jeans and shirts I was just nothing like them at all my room was bare and bland and I had loads of books and just a few clothes hanging up in the wardrobe my bed was always made and my bedroom floor always hovered it was just who I was which my father thought very strange and just too effeminate for him.

I would wander the school grounds on my own and just watch the others having fun and avoid my brothers and his friends like the plague when my brothers friends did see me they would chase after me and pick me up and throw me onto the grass where I would go head over heels my brothers would just look at me and walk away sometimes they would say "oh leave the poor guy alone" I would get up off the grass and brush the dirt and grass off me and just walk around the school with my head down and my trousers wet and grass stained. I would then wait until school finishes to be tortured again at home around the dinner table by my own family.

By this stage my confidence and self esteem and self worth was non-existent again if they were ever there at all I often wondered what happened at such a young age to be inflicted with all of this pain growing up and would the pain ever go away was it because my grandparents died when I was such a young age did grief do this to me was it coming from such a male macho family with so much noise and testosterone I just did not know why I had so much pain in my life at such a young age and life was about to get much much worse for me.

There was a lot of fear in my life from a very early age and as I say I do not know really where all of this fear came from its very beginnings are we born with fear? Or does fear come into our lives through circumstances? I don't know but one thing I did know it was with me and it was growing inside me and getting bigger and bigger every day of my life!

I would wake up every day and think how every day was just so much the same for me I would do the same things every day that it was almost a routine not a quality of life but a life of a routine that I was sick to the back teeth of and I had not even reached my teens yet.

It was especially difficult for me during the summer holidays when the weather was boiling hot and I could hear kids and people outside my bedroom window having fun and laughing and enjoying the warm air and weather while I was hiding away in my room believing that hiding away from the world was the best thing to do in my situation or what I thought was a situation.

I would hear my brothers getting ready to go out and have fun with their mates they would just throw on a tee - shirt and shorts and flip flops and off they go not to be seen again until later tonight while I was sat on my bed in my room with a big wooly jumper on and track suit bottoms and I would run to the window and watch my brothers walking away from the house with their mates and girlfriends all in summer clothing and looking so relaxed and cool with not a care in the world. I would quietly walk over to my bed and think about how sad and lonely my life was and why was I inflicted with all of this pain inside and out and why was I so different to what seemed like every other person in the world.

My mother would shout up the stairs "I am going to work now Nick there is food in the fridge and plenty here to eat ok" I would then hear the front door close and the house empty my dad in work my mum in work and my brothers gone for the day I would probably have no contact with anybody until later tonight when the sun was going down and the sky red and the air cool ' the summer nights ' I did enjoy being alone for obvious reasons wouldn't anybody with my very loud and full of testosterone family but every day during the summer was the same just me and the empty house.

I would try and find things to do to occupy myself which mostly included me watching DVD's all day but I would clean the house and help out my mother as best I could as my brothers and my dad would just make more mess for her which she would clean up without any fuss after doing a full day's work in a busy store.

I had no pride in myself or my appearance at all I walked around in baggy clothes that I had worn for weeks at a time I did not bath or shower I could not be bothered to clean my teeth my personal hygiene growing up was getting dressed and splashing my face with cold water and that was about it every day was the same and I dressed the same too I just could not be asked to clean myself up or make an effort as my brothers did all I could think was what is the point when I just wonder the house all day doing the same thing.

My dad would come home from work first and I would hear his keys in the door and I would sit up properly and act "like a proper man" he would throw his shoes on the floor which were often covered in mud and sit in the arm chair and look at me with his miserable frown and cold stare he would say the same thing every day to me which was "so what have you been doing all day then lying on the chair watching a load of shit I suppose as usual" I would say "no I have been cleaning for mum" he would make fun of my voice and repeat me in a childish manner and say "I have been cleaning up for mum" (you can now see where my brothers get this from) he would put his face next to mine and say in my ear "why don't you get in the bath take off those fucking stinking clothes go and clean your dirty teeth and get out there and get some friends and some girls after you like your brothers, where did you come from ay you couldn't have come from my stock". I would feel my heart beat beating out of my chest and my colour fade from my face I was petrified of my dad and didn't he know it and he made sure I knew it.

My dad was hard on all of his boys but especially on me because I was so different to the others and I think he thought that by being tough on me would make me tough and make me into one of my brothers but all he was doing was making me hate him and making me hate myself.

I did hate myself and my life and my family well apart from my mother but she was no match for a house full of very hard men who made my life a complete misery on a daily basis my life was already tough enough and a steep enough hill to battle everyday without my family adding to it I was twelve years old and I already had thoughts of suicide because then I would be out of so much pain.

I would hear mum and dad arguing about me in the bedroom in the nights and I would hear dad saying "your molly coddling the boy into a girl look how different he is to the boys" and I would hear mum saying "yes he is different and I will love him all the more for it, our son is different and what does it matter why are you being so hard on him all the time", dad would say "I am embarrassed by him I am ashamed of my own son do you get it now woman I would then hear him say" if he is 'if he's one of those a bender I just cannot accept that not one of mine never not in this house". My brothers would walk into my room and say "you caused this argument again why did you have to be born". At this point I would put my pillow over my head and my body would go cold and limp with fear because I pretty much knew even at the tender age of twelve that I was developing into the guy that my dad would not accept and not just my dad the community I lived in and my brothers to boot (oh no).

Here I was finding life hard to grasp and every day was a struggle and I was fighting my sexuality just to make life even more difficult if this was possible what is a boy to do?.

I would wake up every day and just stare at the ceiling and wonder what today will bring for me just more pain and more fear and my body would go cold at just the thought of leaving the house for me it was out of the frying pan and into the fire walking in a world I had nothing in relation with and a world I hated for obvious reasons.

I would not bother with any of the other kids in school I just did not have anything in common with them at all I found them strange and they certainly found me very strange I would wander the school grounds in my coat and hood and try to hide under it like a comfy blanket.

Then on parents evening the school brought up to my parents that maybe I should go and see a child Psychologist because of my constant Isolation and lack of social skills and my personal Hygiene and my parents spoke to the teachers about their concerns about me too so I was transferred to a child psychologist a person I really did not want to see I was very ill a week before the appointment and physically sick and I felt seeing a specialist was just making me feel and look more different and strange than I already was.

The day came to see the child psychologist and I was sat by the doctor with my parents behind me and the focus was on me we discussed over a 7 week period how I should make more time for me and talk more to my parents and how they should make more time for me and how we should communicate more away from my brothers.

We discussed me joining social groups and getting out more with people of my own age and taking more pride in my appearance, the doctor told my father to talk to me more and maybe not be so tough on me but my father reacted by telling the doctor not to tell him how to run his own ship.

It was part of my dad being in control of his family he had deep control issues and used them over me.

One day after week 5 we left the doctor's office and got in my dad's car and my father told me to sort myself out and how all this doctor shit is a waste of time and how I just need to harden up and get on with things communication and sympathy off my dad was just not there while my brothers got on with life I found life extremely difficult with a very aloof father who did not want to understand me and a mother who tried her best to over compensate for this only to get grief off my dad for doing this.

My parents thought it best to send me to my aunt's house on a weekend it was not far away but they both went out on a weekend and my brothers would have their friends over who I did not get on with so they thought it best to send me to my aunt's every Friday until Sunday I did not think this was fare for me to leave my own house but my parents were adamant about it.

My aunt was a very strict older person she was a lot older than my mother and this was all I wanted to be around an older person with strict morals as you can imagine this did wonders for my self esteem and confidence on a weekend was just me and her sat on the sofa watching weekend TV with me worrying about my bedroom back home being invaded by my brothers crazy friends oh my life is wonderful. I would sit on the chair next to her and think what the hell am I doing here I was now in my teens and living the life of a contacourus oap worrying about tomorrow and full of anxiety and having deep issues and problems that I was keeping dormant because I thought if I do this it will keep other people happy but what about my happiness and what about my quality of life.

I told my parents I wanted to stop going to my aunts because I was just bored there and she wasn't exactly fun to be with but constantly moaned about everybody and everyone and I did not need this in my already very unhappy and miserable life. My mother said ok but you know me and your dad go out on a weekend and you will have to put up with your brothers and their friends my mother just told me to stay in my room and keep out of their way. I agreed.

Then one Friday as usual my parents went out and the next thing a knock at the door in walks about twenty of my brothers friends the music goes on and they get drunk it comes to a point in the night where I leave my room to see what is going on one of the lads had been sick all over the stairs and there was food and mess everywhere so in anger I tell them all to get out shouting and exploding at my house being treated in this way and my brothers not caring because my dad just thinks it's boys being boys.

They pick me up as high as they can until my head hit the ceiling and they drop me like a hot potato onto the coffee table which I scream out in pain because I fell on my arm and I could not move it and my body was sore I screamed as my brother tried to move my arm and tell me "not to mention this to mum or dad" but my arm was either sprained or broken one of my brothers friends said "he needs to go to the hospital you fucking idiots you just dropped him like a rag doll", I could just hear them laughing and then they said "I think we had better go", One of my brothers friends called his girlfriend and she took me to accident and emergency where I had sprained my arm and bruised my back.

We got back from the hospital and my parents were furious my father was putting the curtains back up on the rail where somebody had pulled them down and my mother was scrubbing the carpets that were full of sick my mother rushed over to me and took a look at my arm and back and my father just said "Nicky get upstairs with your brothers I don't want to look at any of you tonight" my mother just gave me a look as if to say just go upstairs and listen.

As I was walking up the stairs my father said "you are to go and stay with your aunt on the weekends you just cause trouble here this has never happened before on a Friday night". I just walked up the stairs with my head down.

I got into bed and as usual cried myself to sleep I was just so unhappy with my life and the way my dad treated me to the others because I was a bit different my body and arm was sore and I was being blamed for something my brothers had done but because they were masculine and "proper boys as my dad put it they could do no wrong I just think he felt embarrassed by me for producing such a different boy.

I had nobody I could talk too or relate too I felt alone and invisible to the world and I often thought that maybe the world would be a better place with me not in it and I thought about suicide many times and how I would be out of so much pain if I went off planet earth but somewhere else that I could be at peace a place where I would have no worries about tomorrow or next week. Life just seemed too much for me to bear and I could not understand how so much pain could be inflicted on me and everybody else my age seemed confident and outgoing and worry free how did they do it? How could life be so care free for them and how did they get to enjoy their youth?

As usual my weeks were painful physically and psychologically I was getting older and now going through puberty too I had a huge breakout of acne my life in school was getting worse through bullying which made me not want to go to school life at home was miserable and scary and life with my aunt on a weekend was something I dreaded because she was getting worse with her moaning and depression. I was confused about my sexuality and I had nobody to talk too it all came to a head when my mind was so negative that it affected me leaving the house and being around people I would tremble and shake and sweat whenever I left the house and I would become breathless and flushed and feel as if I was going to collapse and I would just find a place to go where there were no people and take deep and slow breaths and I would get tears in my eyes because I just felt could this life get any worse and why was this happening to me.

The bullying in school was getting worse I reported the guy in question but he just got me back worse for it by psychologically torturing me in class everyday which can be worse than physical bullying my confidence and self - esteem were gone altogether and my dad and my brothers either just ignored me or if they did talk to me would run me down and my mum and dad constantly argued over me because my dad blamed my mum for wrapping me up in cotton wool and I was full of tension panic and anxiety which showed one day when I was having food at home with the family and I could not breathe all of a sudden my chest felt very tight and I felt as if I was being suffocated I ran away from the table not being able to talk but I could no longer sit there I did not want to make a fuss so I just walked upstairs petrified because I could not breathe and I was very scared because I thought I was dying and I thought I was going to collapse my body was soaking wet and I thought I was going to wet myself or even worse.

As I got to the top of the stairs my breathing came back and my body felt limp and relaxed again and my chest was not constricted but loose but I was still sweating and soaking wet I ran to the bathroom and splashed my face with cold water and wondered what the hell had just happened to me and it made me wonder was I even human?.

My mother knocked on the bathroom door and asked if I was ok I let her in and explained to her very quietly what I had just experienced she immediately said "oh Nicky

you just had a panic attack due to anxiety she said it was something she suffered from and still does".
I now lived in fear of getting another one of those because it was the most terrifying experience I had ever had in my young life and again I just thought why me or why me!.

My mother asked me if there was anything I wanted to talk about with her anything at all something that would just be between me and her she would always say "you can talk to me Nick ok" but she was not a strong enough person to battle with my dad over me and I just did not want to cause more arguments between her and my dad concerning me so I thought the best thing I can do is to remain quiet and keep my problems to myself something which over a period of time can have detrimental consequences later on and didn't I already have the symptoms.

I would be sat with my aunt on a Friday night thinking how I should be out socializing and going clubbing and enjoying myself like the others were from school and my brothers and his friends and well finding out who I am and meeting others who I have loads in common with and talking and communicating and falling in love and just simply enjoying being young and loving my youth or just simply not worrying about tomorrow or next week or leaving the house or being anxious all the time but just letting go and having no stress or worry or fear.

I did not know how to exist being happy and having fun was just too much effort for me to do and to walk into a night club or social scene was just panic thinking about it and I could not make out why I behaved the way I did I guess it was internal and external factors which contributed to my worries it would have been nice to have had friends away from home somewhere to escape and just be myself but I did not even have that.

I was now 16 years old my acne was getting worse life was getting harder (if that was possible) and my sexuality was worrying me because I had a huge crush on the head boy of my school and his best friend whenever I would see them my heart would pound out of my chest and my breathing very rapid and my colour blood red I would try not to show this but it would just take over me because it is just the body's way of finding somebody attractive I guess and with me it was guys hot guys!.

I was a scruffy greasy bit smelly spotty teen who was extremely unpopular and these guys were hot attractive well cut cute boys who were very popular what chance did I have anyway even if they were like minded to me which I don't think they were a lot of guys experiment in their youth but it was something I was not going to find out with these two especially not in school and I was in no way myself ready for sexual contact with anybody I could not talk to people let alone have sexual contact with people.

It worried me everytime I would see these two guys around school because my colour would flush red and my heart beat would pound out of my chest and I did not want this to show through I remember one christmas being sat by them and others around our school christmas tree and I thought well here we all are sat together and I was tense and I felt as if I should not be sat here because these people are the popular people and confident people and I have no right being here but one of the guys introduced us to each other and they just said "alright to me" and I responded with "yes alright" that was the only ever contact we had with each other during our school time together but I still remember fancying them as a teenage school boy and I guess this is the body's way of telling you who attracts us and what we go for (some would call it self-awareness) but as I say I never put that into practice due to pure fear.

I was going through a phase of having feelings for certain girls and I could not make this out I was pretty sure I was gay because your body just tells you what or who you find attractive but there were girls who were close to my family and friends with my brothers who I would often look at and have erotic thoughts about and this really confused me.

These girls would come to family parties and family engagements and they would dance alongside me and my dad would say "you're in there Nick go for it" and I would just look to the floor and my mother and me would look at each other I would then look at my dad and I would see his eyes roll as if to say what the hell is wrong with him why has he got to be such a moron and strange boy.

I wanted to sleep with girls and I wanted to see if a girl's body was for me and if this did turn me on after all there was some feelings there and one or two of the girls I could have slept with the opportunity was there I mean these girls were man eaters but a sexual experience with a girl could have been there but I was just in no way ready for this with a guy or a girl I was not ready Psychologically or physically or emotionally I was just a petrified timid very emotional confused guy who was having a lot of deep issues Internally and externally and I felt isolated and I felt as if I needed to please my family all the time I mean my dad wanted me to sleep with girls because it would have kept him happy with doubting my sexuality but I thought the best thing to do is to stay away from both sexes on all levels even as friends this way there is no temptation to test my sexuality and I have not got to get anybody else involved in my problems and my issues. (Big mistake I hear you say and yes I did make a big mistake by thinking and living my life this way).

Life did not get any better for me in fact things were getting worse (could they get any worse I hear you say), at the end of my teens I was still living a fearful life at home I was full of fear and Insecurities my acne had got much worse maybe due to stress I had a part time job but because of my lack of confidence and self - esteem I was having a really hard time from the person in charge and this person was bullying me and giving me a hard time simply because I allowed them too if they said jump I jumped I guess being a walk over at home becomes part of everyday life in other aspects too I just got by day to day as best I could.

I would wake up and the first thought of the day was fear of leaving the house, fear of walking to the bus stop, fear of meeting people, fear of sitting on the bus, fear of going into work, fear of being made fun of in work, fear of doing my duties there, fear of finishing work and walking to the bus stop, and fear of going home to being made fun of and run down by my brothers and my happy dad being so proud of having a son like me and watching my mother obey my dad just like I did I often wonder how she ever married him but I guess it was down to circumstances like a lot of marriages maybe back then he smiled and was fun and had some humanity about him.

My brothers started dating strongly and were not home much and their girlfriends would come over to our house and I was so jealous and envious of them having love lives and they even dated the 2 girls that I had a crush on or I had something on I still couldn't work that one out and sometimes the girl I found attractive would be kissing my brother and looking at me the same time as if she was saying well you didn't want me so I got with him.(I would often think how an earth can she kiss a guy with such a smelly bed such dirty pants and such smelly socks but I guess girls kind of like this about boys).

My dad loved his sons falling in love and being happy and they would come over and he would laugh and joke with them but I could never have that with him because I was pretty sure he would never welcome a guy that I may bring home someday like he welcomed the girls simply because he was homophobic and afraid of his child being different.

I was just a slave to my brothers when the girls would come over and my brothers would say "Nick go and make some coffee's and make yourself useful" and I would hear them laughing about the way I dressed and the way I walked and I would hear my brother saying "he's so abnormal" I would be full of anger and resentment inside because I felt like a complete nobody and invisible to everybody and again I would think would I really be missed if I was no longer here in fact would it be a relief to my family.

I continued to go up to my aunts on weekends where she would moan about everything and we would watch weekend TV and she would say "bloody gay's on TV should not be allowed" homophobia seemed to be everywhere and I could not make out whether they were saying it to tell me something or whether they were just ignorant bigots.

My mother would phone my aunt to see how I was and my mum and aunt would mention the girl I had a thing for just in conversation and I would tremble in the chair at just the sound of her name and this really frustrated and angered me because I knew I preferred guys but why this reaction about the girl it confused the hell out of me.

I wanted to go out clubbing and find out what the social scene at night was all about and what went on and what people clubbing got up to and making friends and having someone ask who is your friend here or somebody buying me a drink just like my brothers did and do and just like the people I work with do what millions of people do to relax and enjoy and dance and have a good time but there was just so much fear to be part of this world and I would be in my aunts spare bedroom hearing people passing the window in the early hours of the morning walking home from the night life and It was then as usual I would cry because the night had gone and once again I had missed out on being part of the clubbing night. (My prince charming had been taken by somebody else once again).

Sometimes I would find it hard to breathe in my sleep and wake up gasping for breath I felt suffocated and alone in the darkness because I was so afraid of life and resentful of others having fun when I was missing out and going through so much pain. I would quietly take deep breaths and try my best to calm myself down and lie on my pillow and try my best to clear my mind and go back to sleep I wouldn't only get this in my sleep but it would also start during the day I guess the pain in my life was taking its toll on my mind and body and I was now in my early 20's.

I remember being sat in with my aunt one night as usual on a Friday and some kids as usual passed my aunts sitting room window and I remember all of a sudden feeling breathless and sweaty and the only way I can describe it is that I wanted to scream out loud as loud as I could ' somebody help me please help me ' I did not do this but my mind wanted to scream out because my body and mind was hurting so much and I was so sick and tired of others having fun and being so full of life and being free of anxiety and fear.

I managed to remain as I was sat in the chair drinking coffee watching weekend TV and looking as I normally look whatever that is bored beyond belief I suppose. I was not well and I knew the way I was behaving was not healthy because I was obviously not happy I needed to admit this to myself and stop fighting and I knew I needed help and I had to go out and seek it what an exhausting journey this was going to be for me.

I planned to make an appointment with my doctor which I did and I went over and over in my head what I was to say to my doctor that I was not well and I needed help but I was scared incase my doctor was to ask me why I thought I needed help but I had to go and see my doctor because I didn't know how much more I could take of my life full of fear on an everyday basis but I was not ready to admit that the problem was my sexuality.

I made an appointment and went to see my doctor and I explained what I was going through and it was getting much worse without mentioning my sexuality so my doctor put me on a list for counseling.

I waited 7 months to see the counselor because they are so busy and in that 7 months I just carried on as normal living a life of pretence and putting a smile on my face while inside I was full of pain and resentment and fear but nobody could have known this because I was so very good at pretence and more often than not acting the wet rag.

I was ok with my life and everyday was the same it was what I was used to being a thousand other people and not or never being me I lost who I was a long time ago and just pretended to be somebody I was not as this gave me strength I used other people to give me strength but it was not healthy to never be yourself because if you do this for long enough your true self can truly disappear and you may never find yourself again time goes on life is short and then we end up very bitter and unhappy in old age too many of us end up this way and regret our lives.

What would rattle my cage and flutter my feathers and make my true colours come out for others to see would simply be other gay men I was absolutely petrified of them I got to learn as I got in my teens and 20's that we know each other through gaydar a kind of secret stare or secret code we have for each other which I think fascinates gay men the world over we just simply know each other and I had always hidden away from this by not going out and not socialising and not going places where other gay men go but doing my best to stay away from them a kind of homophobia coming from a closeted gay man and I would find myself giving gay guys stinking looks as if to say ' you have no right to be gay and open about it ' but it was all resentment because they were just being themselves and getting on with their lives and going with their human instincts and I was punishing and stopping my body doing this and the consequences were proving overwhelming for even a strong minded person like me.

I would have no contact with the outside world apart from my place of work that was where I would have to meet and greet people, from work I went straight home and to my room from my room I would go to my aunt's house and it was painful sometimes to even walk the streets because of my social phobia just walking to work or home or to my aunts it seemed such an effort and brave thing to do for me just to walk anybody would think I had just gone through a life threatening assault course and survived it I then worried about tomorrow when I would have to be seen in public again and I would pump up my negative mind and worry about tomorrow.

Out of the blue a gay man (openly gay man) would come in to the place where I work and I thought ' oh no ' I straight away knew he was gay he was what we call (very camp) and straight away he was asking questions about me to my work colleagues because he knew straight away and I just knew he was going to be a problem for me.

I tried to get control of myself and act strong and try to be nice to him because I did not want people to see that he bothered me but I thought if I be nice to him and act natural around him then people will see he is not a problem for me and that he was wrong about me.

For the first few weeks he kept coming into where I work and at first I got control of myself I did not fancy him but I was envious and resentful of him because he was being honest and I was not he was a screaming queen but he was being honest and not living a life of fear. A couple of people I know did tell me that he had had a word with them about me and told them I was gay which I responded by saying ' what is he talking about ', it was from this point that it was confirmed to me that he knew and he had told people that that he knew I was gay he said apparently "we know each other" I knew this day was going to happen he was just far too comfortable with his own sexuality to keep quiet about me because in his eyes he just did not understand me and who could blame him as I did not understand myself.

From that day on I hated him coming in to my domain and rattling my feathers and keeping on about my sexuality I could not stop him coming in to my place of work but I could do my best to show him how very unhappy I was with him behaving like this and In a way being very cruel to a guy in my ' well situation '. I ignored him and showed him how much I did not like him but whenever I came into contact with him my body would tremble and I would feel as if he had got the better of me because he seemed to have a constant grin on his face and it was as if he enjoyed seeing me so wound up because he knew he had got to me. He went out of his way to make friends with all of my work colleagues and we just ignored each other which people noticed the effect he was having on me. I tried my best not to let this happen but it was becoming a little war of wills between me and him and it was just more stress and fear to my already painful life.

I would find myself dreaming about him and waking up in cold sweats because of him and worrying about seeing him the following day when my body would tremble and the anxiety would start and he would find it very humorous. I did not know how much more of this I could take before my breaking point came but once again my strength came from somewhere because as the weeks and months passed I managed to cope with him and his wicked ways until he stopped coming in to my domain I got to learn he would be one of many. I later got to learn through organisations that openly gay men should never ' out ' closeted gay people because it is just cruel of them as they have no Idea the pain we go through every day and it just makes closeted homosexuals afraid and uncomfortable in the work place.

With all of this going on I was having counseling sessions which I found exhausting because I was not ready to be honest and talk about my sexuality I could not tell my doctor about my sexuality or my counselor we touched on my sexuality with counseling and we spoke about it but it was at a very shallow level and even though the councilor was trying to get it out of me I was fighting to hold it back something I was very very good at because I had spent most of my life doing this. Therapy only works if you are willing to be honest and meet the therapist half way and I certainly was not I was just so used to being in denial and fighting who I was that it became part of me and I was not ready to talk about it with anybody.

I could not think of any other way of living my life without fear being a huge part of it and I was still fighting myself everyday and allowing the fear to balloon and become who I was. When I woke up from bed I could smell fear I could taste fear I could feel the coldness run through my body at the thought of getting up and living another day of fear and my mind would be negative as soon as I opened my eyes I think I might have invented fear as I was living fear the fear that had been there since I was a child had now grown up with me into a young man.

I would think about leaving the house (fear), I would think about my social phobia (fear), I would think about my sexuality (fear), I would think about my family (fear).

I would think about spending the weekend with my aunt (fear) I would think about the dinner table (fear), I would think about the girls name being brought up and me trembling (fear), I would think about life in general (fear). Everything I thought about was negative and full of fear and I could see no way out of it and I felt as if I was the only one going through all of this trauma. A lot of old people go through this when they lose their independence and become lonely and vulnerable just afraid of life but I was finding this at a very early age and I had not even reached old age yet.

How do people fall in love? How do people make friends? How do people have social lives? How do people have sex? How do people enjoy themselves? How do people become confident and happy? How do people get popular? How do people wake up and enjoy their day? All of these things which should be such a natural progression were all fearful and very complicated to me and I could not work out why how I found life so very hard to get through and I was clearly very very unhappy.

I decided to leave my job as I was very unhappy there but my bad luck or the life I was leading was following me around where ever I went and I just could not seem to stop myself being labeled.

I guess the way I stood and the way I presented myself and my closed body language and nervous disposition gave me away straight away that was even before I opened my mouth with my trembling voice. Other people with confident and extroverted personalities just saw me as strange and laughable and not to be taken seriously just like school as I say I stayed the same since I was a small boy and what I went through in school stayed with me into adult life and into the world of work. If you are different it is human nature for people to treat you as different no matter the age.

I tried to be taken seriously and did my very best to be deemed as ‘ normal ‘ and one of the human race but it seemed the harder I tried the more people laughed it was just that I was different to others from a very early age and this stood out to others and I stood out to straight and gay people because the way I lived my life was different and I guess people living in the ‘ real world ‘ could not understand or comprehend why I was being the way I was and neither could I!.

I could not understand or work out how gay people mostly young gay people were just gay they just came of age and accepted who they were and that was that they had gay friends and straight friends they were ‘ out ‘ to their family and friends it was just a natural progression but how do you get that "natural progression" and be so comfortable with who they are and what an earth did their parents think?. I would stop and stare at young gay people and think how do you do that and where do you get the courage from and where is the fear?

I would spend my days walking about during the time I was out of work I tried my best to get out of the house everyday because I knew being enclosed in an empty house all day was no good for me and I was bored and lonely. I would leave the house very early and be the first person out and just walk to our local town and just think about things and watch people with friends and people going to work at least I was around people and out of my room and walking was good for my confidence and self - esteem I would always feel better going back to the house because I had made the effort to leave the house and for me it was an effort but I made myself do it If I panicked when I was out of the house with my ' social phobia ' I learned to control it (I think).

My father was not happy at all about me finishing my job and he said "you should have stuck it out" but the pressure there was just too much for me and I always felt ostracized.

I was now in my early 20's and I decided to go to university and study it would be a chance to be around people of my own age and maybe I could even make friends and get myself a life. I enrolled on a course and told my family around the dinner table what I had enrolled on in university and my dad just said "oh Nick what is the point you need to get proper work and start earning money not do a poncy course" and my brothers just laughed and said "our Nicky in university" it was no wonder my confidence was rock bottom I think it all starts with the family. I did not make friends in university but found myself staying away from the other students especially the gay students because I did not want to be associated with gay people (closeted homophobia) because I did not think of myself as gay so why would I want to be around them and even when I had to be around them which was hell for me I just put on an act and looked stand offish as if to say well I am not gay so what are you looking at.

My look and stare and body language was enough to keep gay and straight people at bay and I was sort of telling them in a non verbal way stay away from me and get lost while trying to be a nice person at the same time.

I would see hot gay guys around the university and found myself looking at them but as soon as they made eye contact I would look away or even give them a killer look as if to say I am not gay so fuckoff. It would leave me feeling rotten and sad with myself (once again the one who got away) they were not hurting, I was, maybe their ego was hurting though maybe.

I could not understand all of this negative verbal and non verbal language and communication I was giving off to people I was just so determined to tell myself I was not gay and that I was into girls and I was confused myself I was getting older and my life just seemed to be getting more complicated and tougher to get through. my parents were still arguing over me because my mother was trying to explain to my father that he should talk to me about certain things but I would hear him yell ‘ what are you talking about woman over my dead body will I discuss that with him ‘, and when gay issues would come on the TV my dad would always say something like ‘ stinking bastards ‘ which would make me flinch and go red and be very nervous and soaking wet and my breathing would become shallow and at the same time trying to show my father I looked natural he never ever said “are you ok what is going on with you” so it was either he noticed and never said anything or he never noticed I was always scared I might have a panic attack and run out of the room one day if something gay came on the TV but I always controlled my breathing and nobody ever mentioned if I was ok they call it fight/ flight I was excellent at fight I was so in control of my emotions that fight would take over but I cannot talk for my legs(they would always twitch and turn to jelly).

I had saved up over 1000 pounds from my last job and I decided to go into the city and be brave and buy myself some gay DVD’s because I was determined to see how the other half live and what gay sex is all about by watching others doing it. I was shitting myself the night before I planned to go and get them.

I was far too shy and quiet to ever experience sex practically and firstly you have to have friends and a social life to get to know people and then have chemistry with somebody and then move on to sex or you can just go out on the gay scene and have casual sex with anybody but these things these natural things were too difficult for me to do because I kept Isolated and I was not happy with who I was.

I was confused I was afraid I was not happy with myself because I just did not want to be gay I did not want these feelings for guys and these sexual urges but neither did I want sex with a woman I just did not know what I wanted. I mean I wanted to be out there clubbing and enjoying myself and sometimes I used to wander city centres on a weekend and watch people out clubbing enjoying themselves after a hard week's work and I used to look very closely at people when I was walking past a club and the thought of me going in there and being part of that sent a cold shiver down my spine and I would have knots in my stomach.

I could have gone out gay clubbing and had a shag with anybody but I was not happy with who I was and I was a virgin in my twenties that sex would have been doing it for the sake of doing it and I could have been used and abused and felt like shit afterwards I was in no way ready to have sex with a guy or a woman I was just a petrified timid and confused guy who wanted to explore my sexuality and find things out but my negative state of mind and fears of the real world outweighed ever going through with being intimate with anybody and this drove me insane.

However I was ready to watch gay porn and I was ready to take that gay porn under my dad's roof the day came to buying the DVD's and off I went that morning to collect them shaking and petrified of being seen buying them and petrified of getting them from the shop to home and getting them home and up to my room I think I trembled all the way to the sex shop and then home which was not really unusual for me anyway (social phobia) but I had done what I set out to do that day and I did I was now the owner of gay DVD's and I bought a hetro one too just to see what both were like.

I continually whenever the family were out of the house got upstairs to put on my porn DVD's which I always loved doing I was definitely more excited by the homo DVD's than the hetro one and when I watched the hetro one I was more excited by the guys than the women so I think this told me what my body was more excited by and how my heart beat would pulse faster when the gay DVD was on I loved watching these guys being intimate with each other because it was so much what I wanted to do but I was refusing my body from letting it take it's natural progression and this was so very frustrating for me. I was taking a huge risk keeping these DVD's in my room and worried everyday in case somebody was to find them and my father and brothers going insane on me or even killing me but it was just a chance and urge I had to risk.

I continued to go to university and found my body and legs trembling more often than not when I entered the university and walked past the other students and I would often feel like I was going to collapse or fall over but I would as usual struggle to keep on walking until I got passed them and I could feel my heart beating or pounding out of my chest and again I would be hot and sweaty and even my scalp would hurt for some reason and I could feel the other students looking at me and laughing and once I heard a guy saying “bent or fucking what boys”.

I went as I did every day to the university I wondered the city on my days off struggled with my confidence and self - esteem when out in social situations and above all else or my whole problem was full of fear and anxiety it just did not seem to want to leave me or get any better and this was really getting me down the one thing that had got better was my skin but I found on bad days it would inflame due to stress. I could not seem to make friends or find love but I felt as if I had a protective bubble around me stopping people from communicating with me and there was nothing I could do about it I would later find out that that bubble was myself keeping people away from me and I was my own worst enemy.

I decided to leave university because I was unhappy there and the place seemed to be full of confident and extroverted happy students and I did not fit that criteria at all in fact I was the opposite. (or did I get off playing the martyr all the time and feeling sorry for myself I think a lot of you would agree with this), but I decided to find a full time job and it would make my dad happy (I was so good at keeping my dad happy or was it pure driven fear).

I was glad to have left university some of the fear had now gone but was I just running away from my problems as usual and was I running away from an Institution which had lots of young people in it who were my age and I was so very scared and petrified to be around people of my age in case they wanted friendship from me or even Intimacy (heaven forbid). I went through a very short phase of thinking I should join a monk's monastery because at least there I would be safe and away from human contact and live for god.

I was now looking for work and in the mean while just spending my days wondering the house watching my secret stash of DVD's which would often leave me feeling frustrated because these guys were having real sex with real other human beings and living in the real world and I was not I was just waiting in fear until my dad and brothers finished work and for them to just fill the house with their booming voices and bigoted views of the world and taking it in turns to fart one after the other and leave the once quiet and tranquil lonely house into chaos and lingering smell. (I so dreamed of getting my own place but I was not brave enough to do this and could I live on my own anyway and could I cope with all the freedom that comes with it the negative mind and Intrusive thoughts fear once again).

When my mother would come home I would just watch her take off her shoes and put her slippers and apron on and she would go straight to the kitchen to make the tea she was just a slave in her own home and she was as miserable as I was but she would never admit it because she was a woman who lived for her family. I often wondered if my dad was jealous of our relationship or did he blame my mother for me being so different. I would try my best not to act too much of a mummy's boy because it would cause arguments between my parents and I did not want my mother to argue with my dad over me as she often did. She wanted my dad to communicate with me more and reassure me about my worries but he was far too much of a man to cope with that and I guess she knew I needed somebody strong like my dad to tell me it's going to be ok and that I have his support no matter what but I knew this would never happen.

I kept on going up to my aunts on a weekend and that really was the only time I left the house apart from work so leaving the house to go up to my aunts was stressful for me because of my social anxieties as I was just a recluse during the week after work. I would rather be with my depressed and constant moaning aunt isn't my life just great than be with my drunken brothers and pissed off father.

I needed to talk to somebody or I was going to explode I was just not well at all and my fear's and anxiety's were on the increase I could see no way out of my very painful and unhappy lifestyle so I needed help but this time I needed to be totally honest and I needed this to work and above all else I needed not to be afraid of other gay men as this was really getting me down especially gay men who I had chemistry with.

I had saved up a lot of money from my last job and decided to seek out private therapy I needed to go somewhere in the city and I needed somebody with a lot of expertise who helps and knows how to help people in my situation I so needed this to work because I did not know what else was next.

I went into therapy thinking I must be honest for this to work I needed this to work and I would go along on days and at times when nobody would notice me gone this was just a very private thing between me and my therapist.

He was a lovely therapist and he said "you have got to trust me and once we get trust as client and therapist we can make this work", we would have a session once a month and every session we talked about my childhood and what happened from there because a good starting point is your foundations but that does and can bring up a lot of emotions and I guess I had to be ready for this it goes deep, and then we would spend some time talking about what had gone on recently and how I felt about some of the things that had gone on. It was so good to meet up with someone and feel comfortable to tell them my problems. Just some of the things we discussed was my social phobias (to breathe through my nose and then exhale out of my mouth and do this very slowly and this can control breathing and walking very slowly and calmly because rushing just makes the heart beat faster and pumps the blood more around the body which can then bring on the body to go into panic mode).

We discussed how I felt about walking past gay people and being in the company of gay people what my reactions would be both physical and emotional and how the panic would inflame if I fancied them and what these symptoms were and how this can be controlled by breathing and not panicking.

We talked about thinking positive to behave positive and try to dissolve the negative in me which let's face it was all of me. The most of it was ' the family ' my environment I lived in and how I felt about that and how the family can have a huge impact on the way I thought about myself and how all of this negativity came about really internally at a very young age which just grew as I got older and how lack of communication and understanding of myself within the family caused me to become withdrawn and hide away from life.

We talked about being in a negative environment day in day out (the family) and me taking on board their views of the world and forgetting or being afraid to air my views and have my opinions but how I preferred to agree with things I found very hurtful towards me just to fit in and look "normal" it seemed I was around negativity all the time and there were no positives in my life, I did not even have a place to go to meet up with people as an escape to meet up with like minded people. I came to realise how important friends are and how not having any can cause isolation and over a period of time I became used to my own company which I was not happy with and very often found frustrating.

My therapist told me what I have been doing is keeping my emotions to myself because you became more and more Isolated as the years went by until in the end you pushed everybody away so much that you got lost and nobody could reach you even I could not reach myself let alone anybody else and it became a way of life but for me this pain I was repressing inside me was having effects on my body inside and out which is not at all healthy. This Isolation becomes universal at home and in the workplace and in life itself other people deem you as strange and non approachable and this is where the Isolation and feelings of low self worth and resentment towards others just stays with you where ever you go. It was just a negative circle of fear which goes on and on and gets worse if not changed by the person going through it but only I could make this change in my life.

It was very deep therapy but I needed change in my life and I needed positivity in my life and I would do anything to make it work because I was hurting inside and out and we all have breaking points even me.

Talking is always the first step and then putting words into action is the second step and after every therapy session I had part of the therapy was to eat in a gay club during the day where I would be around gay people and straight people and this would hopefully take my fears away little by little and get my negative mind to be positive around gay and straight people. All of this was just a negative mind that had built up over many many years simply because I had allowed it too I was not going to be fixed over night but I was trying my best to become the person I wanted to be just free from my fears and Insecurities and I wanted to enjoy life just like everybody else seemed too there was little chance of being chatted up by a gay guy in the day as there was by night so I felt safe and protected by day and ate my food thinking I am not gay I just love the food here that's all.

I was now 28 years of age I had spent 3 years in therapy and was on medication as well I loved all the therapy and I loved all the talking once a month every month over a period of 3 years nobody knew I went there it was just my little escape where for an hour a month I could be myself just simply myself. I was still very unhappy at home and I was still living the life I was frustrated with and fear was still a huge part of me. I got a full time job in a court as a court usher but the fear of openly gay solicitors and barristers and general people who worked there was still frustrating for me because I was still nervous around them and some days I would have to walk around the courts to take messages to the people who worked there and once again my legs would tremble and I would feel like a complete idiot and I could not understand why I would shake like that but it was just my mind being very cruel to me as it always has been.

The thoughts would always be with me of me no longer being here on planet earth but finishing my time here and being in peace somewhere away from all of this pain but some strength inside me would keep me being strong and it would get me through tomorrow but where this strength came from I do not know fight / flight.

For some reason I stopped crying the crying at night stopped I think my eyes were run out of tears and just dried up maybe my crying days were over because I had got through all of the pain and survived it and the real beginnings of hurt had passed maybe the worst was over and my body was telling me that the numbness of all the pain was just there and my body was used to it now it was a way of life to be in pain everyday and I knew no different.

How do I live without pain and fear in my life? And would I survive a life without pain and fear and most of all would I survive a life with just being me whoever me was?

In therapy we talked about me getting my own place away from most of my fears and anxieties but Intrusive thoughts of being away from fear scared me so much because would I do bad things with having so much freedom and I would not have to explain my movements to anybody and could I cope with this. I did not know what to do or feel about being away from fear because it was such a huge part of who I was. (My family or "the family" kept so much fear running through my veins that I thought could my blood and veins and heart possibly live without the symptoms of pure driven fear.

I decided to be very brave and take a chance and get my own place I kept telling myself I am ready!

It almost killed me to tell my own parents but I did it simply because I wanted to.

They were absolutely fine about it in fact my dad was glad to get shot of me and in his own way he was kind of proud of me for standing on my own two feet. The problem was mum but I reassured her it was totally what I wanted but I was scared (scared you I hear you say never).

I loved having my own place and it was strange to have my own space and for the first time in my life I had total freedom and I was petrified of all this freedom because something I had wanted for so many years was now with me and it was scary because I did not know what to do with it or how to cope with it I did not have to come home to a grumpy and fearful dad and four boisterous and loud brothers and a mum who was a bit of a wet rag herself who just fussed over me because she felt guilty that she was not strong enough to put my father straight he was the boss and he knew it.

I was away from fear at home and it felt great but took a lot of getting used to and so did the peace and quiet all I could hear now was the sound of my own TV and my own bodily noises instead of others burping and farting.

I have to admit that even for me it could get lonely and too quiet it is ok now and again but loneliness does set in after a while even though Isolation was a huge part of my life anyway but yes I have to admit I was lonely and there was nothing I could do about it.

The Job I had in the courts there was still a lot of fear there because some people I worked with knew about my sexuality through (gaydar), and as usual this scared me to death especially when some of the guys used to look at me and smile or wink or stare or I would hear them ask as I shakingly walked by ' and who is he ' and I would think or no not again why me!. But I would hear the people I worked with say "oh him well he's very strange and a loner and I think in the closet" I would hear this and then I would see them laugh and this would make me angry and upset because they had no Idea how hard it is for me living the life I lived even gay guys found it very funny which upset me even more.

My defenses would set in and whenever I saw the people who were asking about me around the courts I would do my best to hide or not come into contact with them and when I did boy did I fall apart but as usual the day would come and the day would go and I would still be the same person.

I also did not have to go up to my aunts anymore on a weekend and listen to her moan and groan about everybody and everyone seven days a week was now mine.

I would often sit in my sitting room and just stare into space and think about my youth and where had it all gone and what had happened to me to want to hide away and suffer in silence and I could not answer myself but that Isolation and suffering stayed with me into manhood. I always thought about missing out on being in love as a teenager with a guy or a girl on hot summer days walking hand in hand with a girl through green parks and long fields and having picnics and laughing and joking and kissing and loving being in love and being hot and sweaty and going through puberty and feeling alive because it is hot and I am with the girl of my dreams which I will remember forever. Or being with a guy and finding out about my sexuality and us going on long walks and being the best of friends and walking up to the woods and hiding in the woods and kissing in secret and touching each other where we are both finding ourselves and our love for each other. I guess this is something the majority of teenagers do and how they find out who they are but mostly this happens in nightclubs I suppose and instead of parks or fields maybe car parks or bus stops but for me this youth did not exist and it came and went in the flash of an eye I mean being a teenager seemed to go on forever for me because it was so painful.

I see teenagers today walking hand in hand or out with friends and I think how I will never get the chance ever again to experience something which should come so naturally for millions of people. I guess a huge part of my thinking was if my dad was to see me being too friendly with a guy he may suspect something and I was too afraid if he confronted me about it so it was best to stay on my own and not bring any attention on myself and I kept this attitude in work too stay by myself and nobody will suspect anything I will play it safe I often feel that in some of my Jobs if I were openly gay I would have been bullied for it I was bullied anyway but for somebody like me to be openly gay too could have made my life even worse and I would not have the courage or confidence to stand my ground and homophobia in the workplace.

But it is certainly better to be yourself in the workplace because it is better for your mental health and you will find you would get on with people better simply because there is no fear of anxieties but again it depends on the person and the job you may be in or profession and you as an Individual you know could you cope with being openly gay in the workplace?.

I had now turned 30 and my life was still as full of fear as it ever was I still lived the same old lifestyle and Isolation and I was still full of anxiety and worry and I was still in the closet and still a virgin I had come out of denial to myself but I was still not in acceptance of who I was and I was not ready to accept my sexuality.

I was still very resentful of others and this just hurt me and me only and I was not very happy when I would hear about some of my work colleagues having relationships and going out on dates because this was something people thought I was incapable of and so did I. I guess if others put you down long enough you begin to believe them.

I would try my best not to show my envy but sometimes it would just shine through because my life was so dull and empty and sometimes guys I thought who were gay I would find out had girlfriends or wives which very often shocked me I would think they are either Bi - sexual or living a lie or straight and I got it all wrong which would very often confuse me. I could have met a girl I suppose and had kids and lived a lie just to cover it up or maybe not with my confidence and self - esteem I don't think I was even capable of that.

My confidence and social phobia was getting worse and my fear of gay men was getting worse and my anxiety levels were really getting me down and I did not know where else to turn so I ended up going to organisations which help people like me but it was not at all as I expected and these organisations main goal was to get me to ' come out ' but I was in no way ready to do this no matter what the therapy or organisation or professional people said to me I was just not ready for self acceptance when asked why it was because I had lived this life for so long and I had been so many people for so many years that I did not want to just become me because I knew who I was and I knew who I wanted to become but not having fear in my life and not being afraid anymore and being happy and living my life scared me more than being safe in the closet a place I had spent nearly twenty years or more of my life had almost always been there and all the fear that comes with it I mean how do I live without this and could I cope not living with this in my life.

I was stuck and there was nothing anybody could do to help me I had gone to nearly every professional and at the end of the day there was only so much they could do to help me the other way out of my problems was totally down to me but how do I become just me and get shot of all of this torture on the human body, maybe it is all down to love and letting somebody into my life the power of love maybe this is what I need but with my walls being sky high I was used to pushing people away from my tower with a huge big stick.

I did not see much of my parents but now it was only my mum and dad and two brothers at home and I think my mother had finally put her foot down with my dad in fact I think she came very close to leaving him and she remained with him only because they sorted out his bully tactics and his attitude in general especially towards me. when they came to my house my dad would say to me "Nick a bit feminine here isn't it how about some proper guys stuff hanging about like football cushion covers or a football rug (like what my brothers had in their room), and my mum would look at my dad and say "Nick it's lovely here just as it is don't listen to your dad and be as effeminate with your house as you want to be" my dad would just roll his eyes and remain silent my mother really did have words with him. I could not believe it when my mother went on to say in front of my dad " it would be great now to have a partner with you here male or female doesn't matter". I just looked straight at my dad in disbelief at what my mother had just said in front of the man she argued with constantly over stuff like this about me he just folded his arms and said "yes would be good with grinded teeth.

Good old mum!

I was now 30 and over and my life was still put on hold even though I kind of knew my parents were kind of ok with me being gay if I ever told them but I was still not ok with my sexuality and I was not comfortable with being gay maybe it was me all along who had the problem with my sexuality and I just blamed others. I just grew up not wanting to be gay but I also grew up not wanting to be straight and I grew up not wanting any friends and I grew up in Isolation and I grew up a very sad and lonely Individual. Maybe it goes a lot deeper than my sexuality and it was me in general just being me who's foundations of life were very odd to say the very least anyway and my sexuality just added to it maybe a strangeness has been there from the very beginning or maybe this is all part of my reason(s) for entering the closet in the first place and suffering the effects.

So my family knew or suspected me, the people I worked with knew but kept quiet about it, the people who I met outside of work or casually knew I was gay, it seems the whole world knew but what was my problem then with not being open about it what was my demons and inner struggle to just be honest with who I was and what was stopping me being just me?.

You have gay people out there who's families disown them or hurt them when they ' come out ' which makes the coming out process even harder for them but they are being honest and being true to themselves and it is something they have to take a chance on. I think If I had ' come out ' in my teens or early twenties when I was still living at home then maybe I would have been beaten up by my dad or by my brothers and thrown out and disowned but I was now in my 30's a fully grown man my family had changed my dad's attitude towards me was well ok much better than it was my mother has always known anyway I feel and she would have loved me anyway unconditionally but there was still no acceptance for me of who I was because I was afraid of letting go of fear and I was scared to be happy because it all comes down to this and ran very very deep with me and I was petrified of letting go of the life I had lived forever a life of driven fear.

It was not my family anymore it was not my work places it was not what people thought of me but it was me I was the one with the problem and it had taken me well into my 30's to realise this because I was afraid to be happy because I had never lived being happy and this scared me more than fear itself because I was used to fear.

There was a new guy in the courts where I worked he was very attractive and there was instant chemistry between us and as usual I thought ' oh no ' but as usual I did my very best to keep away from him and not make eye contact with him and if we did make eye contact I would give him one of my killer looks as if to say stay well away (my defenses) he found my situation very funny and I would see him laughing about me with the others I worked with and I would hear him saying stuff like ' what a sad miserable bastard he is and stuff like here comes the oldest virgin in town he thought I could not hear him but I could I would leave work feeling humiliated and resentful and tearful because he had no Idea the pain I was going through probably something he had never experienced I guess it was his way of getting back at me.

I had to try my best to like him and feel comfortable around him but sometimes my legs would start shaking and my anxieties would get the better of me and I hated this so much and I hated my body for letting me down and letting my mind be the stronger one. It was as if he had got the better of me by my body feeling nervous and anxious around him because I knew he knew and there was chemistry there for us both but there was no way I was letting down my defenses never have and never will!.

But I would always fight my body on this and I would get through the day some shape even if I did look like the court jester and I often felt like the court jester compared to the others I worked with who seemed to have happy and healthy lives both in work and out of work maybe I was my own worst enemy and maybe it was time to nip this life of mine in the bud once and for all but how?.

I loved having my own place so much but it was certainly quiet enough for a lot of reflection of myself when I was at home with the "family" I was very unhappy and scared most of the time but that fear kept me away from my thoughts of work (the only outside intervention I had with the world) and there was enough fear at home without thinking about work too but now it was just me and my thoughts and there were a lot of thoughts during these nights sat on my own thinking about how sad my life is and how lonely I was and how I came to hate people because I resented them for resenting me.

These guys who fancied me could not have me and that must have drove them insane because this was not a nightclub environment relaxed and easy and at times sleazy, this was a professional environment where we all had to respect others whatever the situation in our personal lives and there was certainly a line you did not cross concerning me no matter who you are.

When the courts were empty and everybody had gone home I would often look around at where the guy who fancied me sat today and where he sat yesterday and just stare at that place and wonder where will he sit tomorrow and will my nerves get the better of me again when I see him and also resentment because maybe I did fancy him and maybe I had lost out once again to somebody else all through my own stubbornness.

As It turned out he had been transferred to another court and I was very sad about hearing this yet glad at the same time sad because maybe he could have been the one and I let him get away sad because he was so right about me I was a sad lonely miserable bastard and maybe I was the oldest virgin in town but he had not got the better of me and I had not fallen into his arms and he was not the one to bring me ' out ' to put a spell on me that would dissolve my closetry I had won the day again but who was the lonely one and which one of us was hurting it certainly was not him was it!.

I would do my very best to go and see my aunt whenever I could as my mother would tell me that she missed me so much on weekends as I was the only person who really went there. Then one day I went to see her and we were both sat on the chair in front of the fire with coffee and biscuits and all we could hear was the clock ticking in the silence of the room and she brought up to me how once she was in love with a very handsome young man who she was going to marry. I was shocked about this as I had never thought she had even dated as she was a spinster. She went on to say that he was the love of her life and how she so much wanted children by him but one day she came home from work early due to feeling ill and to her total astonishment found him in bed with his best friend who was a man.

I almost tipped my tea on my lap because I did not expect her to tell me this and nobody ever spoke about this before I did not know what to say and just looked into empty space in amazement.

I said "a guy and you had no suspicions at all that there was something going on between them" "nothing at all she said it was a stunning shock we both talked after he managed to calm me down and apparently the feelings for him outweighed his feelings for me last I heard he had moved abroad with him but that was a lifetime ago but he broke my heart alright and I have never bothered since". "she said I never mention his name I never talk to his family and I asked your mum and dad and other family members to never mention this part of my life to anybody."

"But why do you now mention it to me I said" my aunt looked at me and said "Nicky my love I have been watching you on weekends sat here with me and me and your mother have been discussing you for years since you were 12 because your mother has been wondering since you were 12 if maybe you were gay" "I said what what but I mean me no way" "my aunt said" the reason I mocked gay people on the TV was to try and get a response from you I was hoping you would shout at me and say oh shut up would you or something like who cares I was hoping to get a reaction from you so we could get talking away from your parents."

She said "I have just said something to you which I have not spoken of for years why don't you open up to me I am asking you to me and your mother want you to be happy and we don't want to see you suffer in silence".

I frowned and looked down to the floor I did not want to let down my fences I wanted to hang on to them because they kept me safe for so many years from questions such as these and circumstances such as these that words were too impossible to come out of my mouth especially to my aunt who I never thought in a million years I would be having this conversation with.

I looked up and looked at my aunt it was such a relief though to be asked to talk about this I was not going to her she was coming to me as my aunt and my mother and this was very brave of her but she was doing it for me and for once in my life I felt human to my family and I felt as if I counted after all. I just said to my aunt "well to be honest I am confused is it a girl I want or a guy or both I really don't know.

My aunt said "ok great a start you see I am human after all (and we both laughed) so the story I just told you about me would you be comfortable and happy settling down with a woman snuggling up on the sofa, sharing a bed, even having sex (I said aunty) I am just being human here Nick meet me half way please I know how the world works you know I wasn't always this way so how would you feel about that what does your body tell you. she went on to say would a woman make you happy or would you resent her and end up hating her and hating yourself even more because you are lying not only to you but to her too and maybe the temptation to sleep with a guy would always get the better of you until you are found out and living a secret gay passion.

“or she said can you see yourself with a guy doing all of the above but with a guy lying on him on a cold winters night with a person smelling of man and talking of man and feeling his hairy arms and touching his beard would you feel more you and safe and comfortable and happy with a guy would that just be who you are attracted more to a man than a woman”.

“you know Nick there is nothing worse than lying to yourself but it would be even worse being with a woman just to keep us happy and things would get ten times worse if you went on to have children this could have happened to me you know but I found him out in time. You have to look deep into your feelings about who you are mostly attracted to and who turns you on the most.”

“It is not so much about sex you know but about feelings and emotions and being true to yourself and you have to search for you and find out who you are best suited to.”

I left my aunts thinking for the first time how she has been a true friend to me and how she is now a link of communication to me whenever I need to talk she had been through so much herself and homosexuality had been the reason for her losing her true love and she shared that secretive information with me to help me because she used that awful situation to reach me at such a deep level and she had some personal experience with it herself.

It was definitely a guy I wanted the most I just knew deep inside myself that this was the true me and other gay men knew it too it does not say that I will never experience sex with a woman because it could just happen at some point in my life it will be nothing long term or serious but it could happen as maybe a one off or it may never happen but I knew where my true feelings were and I knew what I was born to be.

Many of you may be thinking do you know you are bi - sexual it is in the text it reads out to us but for some reason not to you. A gay man would never feel he could perform sexually with a woman unless he had bi - sexual feelings? But how do you explain then guys who try gay sex when they are younger? How do you explain women who have lesbian experiences? These guys go on to have families and settle down but it was something they tried once and their wives may never know about it. And the women were lesbian once and are now with guys you know how do you explain all of these feelings and emotions that is why we have LGBT because this covers all this.

You know the old saying never mock it until you have tried it well for lots and lots of people this is not true they never will try it not in a million years I would call them 100% hetro and that is that!. But for the rest of us the sky is not the limit right and who can explain it the only explanation we have is this just makes us human.

So I think that was how I worked out me in the end or did I work me out (who knows), but for me it was definitely a guy I knew that was where my true feelings were but I would never rule out a chance encounter with a woman it did not happen at a teenage age but it could happen at a late development age and maybe that is where the girl in question comes into this because I missed out on a sexual encounter with her but I would never rule out a sexual encounter not with her but maybe with the female species. - I bet many of you are screaming at this book your Bi - sexual man especially you 100% homosexual who can explain it.

My other two brothers had now also left the family home they had house shared with friends of theirs so it was now just mum and dad and the house my mother would phone me and Invite me over for dinner and it would just be us 3 around the table which felt odd but my dad wanted me to come around more often as I think parents tend to chase you as kids get older and they get older funny how it works that way but I guess the damage has already been done by then.

I still felt a bit frosty with my dad even though he was trying his best to be a good dad to me and I think he felt guilty about trying to make me into something I wasn't as a kid but maybe his intentions were good or were they just very selfish but he was my dad and he was trying to redeem himself with me I think.

I changed jobs once again and went to work for a multi story shopping center with thousands of staff well ok it seemed like thousands of staff I was now 32 and approaching 33 and all of my nervous symptoms were still with me (do you think they ever leave you?) and fear was still a part of my life it was hugely reduced but it was still a huge part of my life too and I was still living with being afraid (does that ever leave you either?) but it was here in this multi story shopping centre that a guy would bash down my door and tear my fences apart (these are my inner demons by the way not any property of the shopping mall), and stand up to me and put it to me straight and show me emotionally and with his own will and determination why I should let him into my troubled and complicated life and his name was Richard!.

I saw him straight away it must have been on my 3rd or 4th day working there and he worked on the 5th floor and I was based on the 7th floor and our eyes met straight away I looked over at him and he kept looking my way I quickly made my way to my floor and thought to myself oh no here we go again but this time something was different about this guy and it was kind of love at first sight.

There were so many people working in this place that I thought I may not come into contact with him again for another month or so it was not like my other jobs where there was constant contact with people this place was humongous and had hundreds of staff. Then on a Friday morning after I had seen him on the Thursday afternoon he came to see me on my floor he must have asked about me and what floor I worked on and he then came looking for me there was nothing or nobody stopping this guy from looking for me or asking me any questions he wanted too to him I was a gay guy that he had gaydar with and it was switched on between us and he was going with his Instincts.

I was stacking some cushions on this Friday morning and kind of looked over because I could feel somebody walking my way and yes it was him the guy called Richard.

He kept walking towards me and was smiling at me as he was walking my way and his reason for this was because I was his target whether I liked it or not, he came up to me and I just froze I had never had anybody walk up to me like this before and he said "hi well I am Richard and I believe you are Nicky" or "yes I said I saw you yesterday on floor 5" "I know you did he said that is why I am here with a chuckle", "ok I am going to the cinema tonight I mean I was going on my own but I would love you to come with me" (my body was tingling and excited because somebody was asking me out with them but my fences were still high and I had to show him who was boss here and who was in charge but I was going to have a bit of a joke with him because I really wanted to go to the cinema with him and I was a little stronger person now than I ever was before). "Look I said why would I want to go to the cinema with you" "well I um well I thought we had a um um you were looking at me and um well"

this was so very cruel of me to put him through this pain he then got angry and said "well fuck you I just thought hey look fuck you ok" and he walked away from me I let him walk for about 2 minutes and then with a grin on my face chased after him "hey rich come here I am joking I am joking I was just joking" "just joking said Richard you twat it took a lot of courage to walk up to you and ask you out I was fucking shaking it's never easy you know" "sorry I am sorry what can I say" me and Richard just laughed "your mad" he said "we can go straight from work if that is ok to the cinema" "yes that is great I said you're on" "brilliant meet you in the lobby at 6.00" "I will be there".

I had finally let somebody into my control freak of a world and this person had walked straight through my defenses simply because I had let him I was still scared and I was still full of fear and I was still unsure what I was doing and insecure about this going any deeper but isn't this everybody who goes on a date don't we all have these feelings and emotions when we first meet somebody no matter what the age or the sexuality.
I could not help thinking what would my father think of this if he knew? What would my brothers think of this if they knew? What would the new people think about this who I work with and the past people I work with who I have shut out? I didn't even know what my feelings were about

this cinema thing tonight but one thing I did know I was going to the cinema tonight and I was going with a guy who I had a deep connection with and this was the start of something for me and I was nervous yet excited at the same time maybe this finally was a breakthrough for me maybe my time had finally come to be happy what can I say it just comes without even knowing it. I had finally had a connection with my own body and mind at the age of 33.

We met in the lobby and off we went I was nervous and Richard was nervous but we had such a deep connection but if Richard had not come to find me I never would have gone to find him but his Instincts for me like an animal on heat made him come looking for me and track me down to the very spot I was on.

We watched the film and as we were watching the film I could feel Richard looking at me and I looked at him when he looked away but every so often we both stared at each other together. We went for a meal after the film as Richard was determined to pay and we obviously got to talk during the meal about each other Richard told me about his life and how he had been with a girl for many years but was seeing a guy at the same time and all the guilt that comes with it and how in the end his feelings for guys outweighed his feelings for any girl and he came clean about his sexuality to his family and his girlfriend who he was living with it was hell for him but he felt he could breath for the first time in years and be himself and not lie to anybody. I said “so you are bi - sexual, oh no he said I just was in denial for years and living a lie “you understand.

He had tears in his eyes talking about his dad because their relationship was not what it used to be and they were very very close before he came out but every day was a new one for them he said.

Then it was my turn oh boy oh my god rich where do I start I said and would he believe it well I said here it goes I am not officially out of the closet yet Richard said “I did gather that”

(We both laughed) “how I said” “well he said your nervousness your body language the way you reacted when I asked you out I know other closet cases you know and your all the same” “it hasn’t been easy I said” “I know he said I know, I have a friend who is not yet ‘out’ so I know all the complications that comes with it.

Richard said “you’ve had girlfriends though yes growing up you must have” “no I said not at all” “you’ve had hidden boyfriends then right” “no I said nothing, nothing at all.

Nobody”. Richard said “so you’re telling me your a 33 year old virgin” “well yes I am” (Richard burst out laughing and said “I don’t know anybody like you”) “well you do know I said” “but what about sexual frustration and curiosity and well being human and having needs” “I have been through it I said this is what fear does to you it controls everything even my sex drive in fact my whole mind and body".

This is where I differ to other closet cases and take it to a much deeper level because I did not date girls to cover it up I did not get married or have children or even have friends but for me this was total 100% Isolation going through closetry it kind of takes it to another level.

"So how on earth did you let me in" "it was just the right time my mind and body just let it happen I suppose" "so do you even know your own sexuality then I mean I have slept with girls and guys but for you well are you that in touch with your own body that you didn't have to try anything" "I am still a little unsure I said but I am more comfortable and safe with you than I could ever be sat here with a woman it just feels right and good and me to be here with a guy well you understand". "of course said Richard and you have to go with your Instincts it did not work this way for me but hey your kind of unique in this world which is great". "a 33 year old virgin though wow".

"so are you scared of sex said Richard" "I said no not at all but it does have to be very special for me because I have waited so long for it to happen and I am not going to rush it", "oh I would not dream of rushing you said Richard" "what makes you think it will be you Mr. arrogant" "oh something just tells me" (once again we both laughed).

I explained to Richard how I want to take things very easy and very slowly and how he would have to be very patient with me and I apoligised for being so pathetic but he understood and he said he would work with me and over time he hoped our relationship would get much much deeper and there would come a time when I could 100% trust him. He was so understanding and maybe this is what he wanted too deep down after his emotional rollercoaster past which both of us had been through with different stories. (it would take us 6 years before I was finally ready to get intimate with Richard and he waited for me to be ready because even though Richard was sexually experienced he too wanted this to be so very special not only for me but for him too it was like his first time all over again too and Richard always said to me if you can wait so can I).

Two years had gone by and I was now 35 and going on 36 Richard was also in his early to mid thirties and we started off as friends and over the two years our friendship got stronger and our relationship deeper we had our breaks together in work and very often went out together after work and I slept over Richards and he slept over mine but Richard knew we could cuddle together in bed but not get intimate with each other because I was not ready to get intimate. I know what you are thinking a huge huge part of a relationship is sex and sex should be nonstop in the early stages of a relationship it should just be sex, sex, and more sex but I wanted to wait until I was ready I mean Richard was frustrated and so was I but I wanted to wait because I knew once it was done and we had had sex then I would no longer be a virgin and I was afraid of that.

We had a very strong bond and we were not just boyfriends but the very best of friends and I could not help thinking and feeling that Richard did not understand me he never let on that he did not understand me but I knew he didn't as I still did not really understand myself.

My mother caught on to the fact I was dating or had a friend because whenever she called the house I was not there and I told Richard to never answer the door or phone if I was not at home for obvious reasons which I know Richard hated. I was not' out' at home or to the family but I was 'out' at work and all our friends and work colleagues in work knew we were an Item and this was fine there was the odd homophobic remark from a couple of the more "macho" staff but you get that whatever the part of the world you live in I hated it but sticks and stones.

Richard told his family about me why shouldn't he? and his mum kept on to Richard as to when she is going to meet me and that she would make a family meal for me sometime but Richard explained me to her and she still could not understand why I would refuse to meet at least his family and Richard was hurt that I would not agree to go and meet his mum, Richards dad was more in the background and just read his paper and had been told to keep his remarks to himself when Richard was home which he had to agree to or get agro from Richards mum. But to me meeting Richards's parents and thinking of them as my family is just acceptance of who I am and I really still felt deep down that I still refused to accept that I was in a relationship with a guy and that this relationship was a gay one. I think I still thought of myself as not gay which is why the thought of sex was totally out of the question for me.

I was worried that during sex with Richard that maybe I would not like it and would Richard be able to control his sexual presence over me if I said stop would he? And how would I feel if I ran out of the room during sex how would that make Richard feel? All these questions were running through my head concerning our sex life which at the moment was dead.

Richard had spoken to his friends about our sex life or lack of it as he blurted it out on my 36th birthday after he had got blind drunk and he said how our relationship was ridiculous and he had hated being a hidden secret from my family and from myself too and how if he wanted to he could move on to find another loving relationship that he would not feel like a complete stranger too. I did not know what to say to him because I was as sober as a judge and all these words he was saying to me were dutch courage and pure 3 years of frustration of living like friends rather than boyfriends I think almost anybody would have blown up by now especially us being fully grown men as well as we were in no way young in love teenagers going through a tiff.

My eyes just watered and I felt so guilty about treating him like an outsider for the past 3 years and he was so right about all he said I was lost for words and for the first time we slept in separate beds in my house as we always hugged each other in bed and talked for hours.

The following day Richard apologized and he told me he didn't mean any of it and that it was just the drink talking and he told me how much he loved me I stopped him saying anymore and told him that maybe he should move on and forget about me and meet somebody else who truly deserves him. He responded by telling me so this is your way of pushing me away I can feel your fences coming up from the ground and pushing me far far away from you this is the old Nick making a comeback. I said the Old Nick maybe the Old Nick has never gone away maybe he has always been there and will always be there maybe it is impossible for me to change.

Richard responded by saying "utter utter shit you want me so badly it hurts and you are in pain so much because you want me but you are afraid to have me because then you'll be happy and you have never been truly happy you need to cut out the shit going on in your head and put a stop to it once and for all and accept defeat of who you are a fucking gay guy."

I said "who the fuck do you think you are" he responded by "your fucking gay boyfriend that is the fuck who I am you got a problem with that gay boy" (I burst out laughing and so did Richard then I burst out crying and so did Richard we hugged each other on the floor and I was exhausted mentally and physically and I seemed pretty much out of fight what more was there to fight? And why must I keep fighting?

Richard thought it a good Idea to go into therapy again but this time we would go together and we could work with a trained therapist Richard knew all about my other therapy and he thought this might be a breakthrough for us he always reminded me that he would stand by me no matter what he was totally 100% committed to me why else would he be with me.

We found a relationship therapist and we worked with her over a period of 3 years and we covered everything in every minute detail she wanted to know everything about us as this is the only way the therapy would work as usual being 100% honest and in our 1 hour sessions we talked about everything and then went home and put those sessions into practice if we had problems with each other we would talk about it and gradually work on it step by step.

We had now been together 6 years and through therapy I went out clubbing with Richard, I met Richards friends, I met Richards family which was terrifying but through therapy we talked about the process and what I was thinking and put those thoughts into positive ones our motto was always positivity and then thinking positive and feeling positive and then putting it into practice it does not make you immune from fear but it reduces the fear to a minute detail and making the process a good one.

I had to keep saying to my mind no negativity no negativity positivity positivity and I was taught how to train the mind to be positive mentally and physically on the body, it did not make me immune from my inner demons but again it reduced the fear and negativity that had total control over my body. Having Richard to help me as well and having someone to talk to and someone to be strong for me away from therapy made an enormous difference to just therapy itself.

My therapist or our therapist kept reminding me how very lucky I was to have somebody like Richard in my life as many other guys would have walked away from such a mess of a person a very long time ago. She would always say to me "he is a gift to you Nicky and you should cherish that".

At the tail end of our therapy as I was turning 39 and Richard was 37 it came to a point where I should ' come out ' to my parents and my family and me and Richard being intimate as I did not want to be a 40 year old virgin I also in therapy came out to Richard that me having sex with a woman could happen at some point in my life that I could not rule it out our therapist mentioned possibly me being bi - sexual and that maybe at some point if Richard allows it of course we could together have a woman join us during sex to see if I enjoy it with Richard by my side if you like a three some with a woman it was an option for us and we were just being open with each other.

Our therapist thought it good to be open with Richard about this as then there are absolutely no secrets in our relationship and I was being totally honest with myself and my partner which by doing this can give me acceptance of myself simply because I am being honest about who I am.

Richard had been totally honest with me from the very start about his life living with a woman and then having sex with guys and finding himself and his true sexuality some people just know through Instinct who they are others have to physically try things it makes us human.

Communication between me and Richard was vital and it was very very important for me to be fully open with Richard about my every thought and every single worry and vice versa and bring these up in therapy too it just made me stronger and made us stronger in our relationship it felt so good for Richard to know my every worry and for him to re -assure me that I was just being negative again and thinking the worst which isn't always a bad thing because the occasion then goes better than expected.

we would go and see Richards parents and again I would think the worst his dad is going to start an argument or something nasty is going to be said and I would tell Richard about my anxiety and he would re - assure me to relax and stop using my over active Imagination and most of the night he would say to me "are you ok, are you ok" and I would respond with "yes, yes.

Richard's mother would say "oh he is so quiet bless him "which would make me blush.

Richard would always say to me nobody will disrespect you or me in my parents' house not my parents or my brother there could be some banter but even I laugh at that you've got to.
I had to tell my parents about Richard me and Richard discussed it and we talked about it in counseling too we all came to the conclusion that the best way to do it is invite my parents to my house and make a meal for us make the mood relaxed and then pick my time and tell them. There would be no interruptions because it would be my place.

I picked the night and the way I was going to tell them we pretty much talked in therapy about how they knew anyway it would be no big shock but it would just be confirmed that's all once and for all. I was a man of 39 years of age and I felt like a boy of 5 because it was so fearful to get the words out.

Me and my parents were sat around my dining room table we finished our food and desert and now it was time there was no way they were leaving my home tonight without me telling them Richard would be devastated and so would our therapist who we called our friend if I did not say anything and Richard was waiting anxiously at home for my phone call to tell him to come over and let him know all.

It was time and I started by saying "ok there is something you should know" my mother sat up and said "oh ok" and my dad just looked at me and frowned as he would I was so used to his frowns. "ok I said something you have argued about me for many years is true (it was like reading from a script that I spent years rehearsing for and finally got the part and had to give an exceptional award winning performance it was a scene I had gone over in my head so many times but was impossible to put into words until now)" well I said it's true about me what you were arguing about when I was growing up, (the award winning script was condensed down to a pathetic my parents have to say it for me because I could not) my mother just said it "oh for god sake Nicky your gay right" my dad leaned back in his chair and looked at my mother and my mother gave him a look that said you dare you bloody well dare. (Which made me laugh)?

"oh so the big mystery is true then I see" said my dad. "yes dad I said it's true and I just came out and said it I have a boyfriend too and his name is Richard "which I said without taking a breath and in mumbo jumbo language but my parents caught it.

The relief was absolutely overwhelming and I could finally breathe and I must have got colour back in my face as I felt my blood drain and then come back I could feel my own colour fade from my face and my lips and mouth go dry.

My mother said "oh Nick we knew love we have always known and it's ok we cannot wait to meet Richard can we my mother said to my dad" my dad said "look Nick I have been hard on you over the years because I thought I could change you and make you more like your brothers to toughen you up but it didn't work did it" "no I said it didn't work". (my dad got up from his chair and hugged me which left me in complete shock and said "you're a man now and you make your own decisions in life if this is the life you want then you have our support"). It had taken me twenty odd years to accept myself and in a way it had taken my parents the same length of time because they knew and they were as scared as I was about it so in a way we all came out together.

My mother said "do you want us to tell the boys or will you" I said "would you both do it" "of course said my mum" "well said my dad there it is then" "there it is then I said" (I did not go into other aspects of my inner demons with them about thinking about women too and bi - sexuality and just deep confusing inner issues with me they would not understand homosexuality was enough for them to understand if they did understand it at all).

I phoned Richard he came over and nearly killed me by asphyxiation he jumped for joy on the outside and I jumped for joy on the inside and it was done!

Richard knew everything about me and I knew everything about him we had been together now for 6 years and we were partners and the very very very best of friends too we were soul mates he accepted my inner issues and he loved me for it maybe I would always have inner issues but he accepted that and accepted me. we had not even had sex yet after 6 years and Richard was going insane about it but he was still with me I was a guy with deep issues and problems that go way way back and I had met a guy that worked with me on it and loved me for it what more could I ask for and how many would have stuck by me through all of this.

Richard had now met my family and they all fell in love with him just as I did Richard was far more confident than me around people and he just fitted in by talking to my dad and my brothers and my mum while I just faded out in the background I think they got to like him better than they liked me in fact I was jealous of him because they just fell in love with him so fast and I was still so nervous around his family. My mother brought up that maybe she should go out and buy an outfit for our wedding and I said

"Mum". When we got back to my place Richard brought up the fact that maybe we should get married for my 40th birthday now everything was ok what was stopping us I just blurted out with ok let's do it.

We decided that we should get married before I turned 40 because I was a virgin groom (can you believe that I can't believe it myself) I did not want to be the 40 year old virgin I never wanted to be the 40 year old virgin and we decided that we would get married while I was still 39 and listen for it we would actually have sex an hour before I turned 40.

Well we told everybody it was short notice but everybody came we got married even our therapist came the day went great for us and the night went great for us it was 10.50pm and me and Richard went unnoticed to our hotel room where listen for it "we had sex yes that is right we had sex" and it was an experience I will never forget it was special for both of us because we were destined to spend the rest of our lives together and we would feel for each other the same in old age as we always have about each other the best of friends, lovers, and soul mates for life how many people get this unique love in their lives with the person they are destined to meet.(I always say he was sent from god).

12.00pm came and Richard whispered in my ear happy 40th birthday to my husband.

(We had made it).

I think Richard always knew I would not be 100% comfortable with who I was or with us but I think he accepted me being me just a complicated person who was as deep as the ocean who over thought everything even life itself.

I was never a sexual person really but Richard thought sex was a huge part of our relationship so I went along with it. I would often stare into space when I was alone and wonder what life would have been like if it had been the other way around if I had been married to a woman with a few kids and been a family man. It would happen when we were out shopping too I would see fathers with their kids and wonder why I couldn't have had that life. But thinking like this was not fare on Richard at all he had been so very patient with me simply because he loved me and I would feel guilty when I sometimes hated myself.

Whether I liked it or not I was being true to myself and I was living my life the best way I knew how with a lifelong partner by my side who was always doing his best to re assure my anxieties that tomorrow is a new day and we must live everyday now like we are teenagers again Richard was certainly the teenager in our relationship.

End

I can always say that I made it to an old man and got through this life with a little laughter in my croaky throat and a tear rolling down my wrinkled face and stare into space and wonder now what is next for me in the other world maybe that is another book for another time and will I over think everything in that life as I have done in this one.

EPILOGUE

This is my story and this is the second version of my story the first time I came out to my family at the age of twenty which is late for the 21st century right but come out I did because it was either lose Richard or come out to my family and because I came out quiet young my family were not ready for it and as you know I paid the price and went through hell. But there was no way I was going to lose Richard and go back to my awful and miserable life to please my family I just would not have been able to cope with it and losing Richard was not an option.

This my second version of my life coming out deals with my story from a much different and very very very deep look that goes as deep as the ocean itself. I felt I should give you a version that deals with my Inner demons and inner convictions and sees me come out through my own convictions at a very very late age and I mention no sex so yes this really is the opposite to my other version in fact in this version I am celibate wow. (ok you people who came out in your teens I am a wet rag and maybe to you this was absolutely silly but do you now see what fear can do to you if you allow it to do the driving have some compassion please and don't make fun of the hour before I hit 40 at least I did it before I hit 40 Oh leave me alone).

In this second version I have my own regrets because I never experienced falling in love as a teenager, I never experienced falling in love with a girl at a young age when my testosterone levels were supposed to be sky high. I never experienced going on picnics in the summer on some beach or out in the country with a girl or a guy growing up and finding myself and having fun these things were all alien to me because of fear and I never experienced friendships and bonding and emotional attachment and sexual awakening all things which should come so natural just like the birds and the bees just a part of human life on planet earth were not natural to me.

My summers and my days growing up were spent hiding behind curtains which I kept half open only allowing a little sunlight into the house and going through some sort of deep depression which I kept hidden very very well. Maybe I could have given my family the benefit of the doubt and opened up to them and asked them for help but I had far too deep Inner convictions which I have explained in deep detail.

So yes these are my regrets and I have to live with those regrets for the rest of my life but all I can do is talk about my regrets and maybe just maybe help other people by telling my story and hopefully showing others that this is not the right road to take it really is not. I will never get my youth back and I am very bitter about this as you can imagine but I am not going to take my anger and my resentments out on others far too many people do this in the world and this is by no means moving on.

I have decided to take the good path and help others by telling others my mistakes and hopefully just maybe hopefully I can make a difference in the world by doing good because there is enough bad in the world and we certainly do not need any more of this do we.

Whichever version of my story you prefer I hope they can make a difference to your lives and help you by reading them as much as they have helped me by writing them because life is far too short for regrets and resentments.

This is not a tablet for a cure for closetry (I wish I could make those tablets and end closetry once and for all but I cannot). All I have done is created a story of closetry and wrote about the symptoms and its effects on the human mind and body.

My hope is that I have done a good enough job here through my writing to put people off going into closetry (if they feel they must) and / or maybe helping others who are going through closetry to feel they are not alone and that this story (unique in its own way and to the Individual) is astronomical worldwide it just goes to show how very different we all are and this just makes us human.

You have to make your own tablet and your own cure and I am afraid only you can do that and you alone but people like me can help by sharing our stories.

Coming out has got to be in your own way and in your own time and you will know when this is your mind will let you know it will happen without you even knowing it will just feel right for you that is why you have to be strong and you have to find ways of coping until you find yourselves.

I do not know what advice to give to you about the coping strategy you know read this story I hope this helps because this is all I can do for you I cannot come and see you one to one individually because I am not super human I wish I was but I am not. But it does get better I know you are frustrated I know I have written a book on the subject but stay with us for the ride it might be bumpy and scary but all rides come to a stop and a flat surface.

I also want and feel I should say something to the people on the other scale to this book the people who have never experienced closetry and think closetry is absolutely pathetic and can see no sense in going through all this shit.

I know you are just out there and living your lives to the full but please be careful and care about your bodies I know you feel Invinsible especially the younger generations but remember to always be sensible and be very careful in all aspects of your health and well being.

Julian Black.

www.ingramcontent.com/pod-product-compliance
Ingram Content Group UK Ltd.
Pitfield, Milton Keynes, MK11 3LW, UK
UKHW040019200726
13854UKWH00001B/270

9 781496 987877